You CAN'T Please EVERYONE!

by ELLEN FLANAGAN BURNS
illustrated by TRACY NISHIMURA BISHOP

MAGINATION PRESS • WASHINGTON, DC
AMERICAN PSYCHOLOGICAL ASSOCIATION

FOR KAELYN, MY SHINING LIGHT—*EFB*

FOR ANDREW—*TNB*

Books for Kids From the
American Psychological Association
maginationpress.org

Text copyright © 2022 by Ellen Flanagan Burns. Illustrations copyright ©
2022 by Tracy Nishimura Bishop. Published in 2022 by Magination Press, an
imprint of the American Psychological Association. All rights reserved. Except
as permitted under the United States Copyright Act of 1976, no part of this
publication may be reproduced or distributed in any form or by any means,
or stored in a database or retrieval system, without the prior written permission
of the publisher.

Magination Press is a registered trademark of the American Psychological
Association. Order books at maginationpress.org, or call 1-800-374-2721.

Book design by Rachel Ross
Printed by Phoenix Color, Hagerstown, MD

Library of Congress Cataloging-in-Publication Data
Names: Burns, Ellen Flanagan, author. | Bishop, Tracy Nishimura, illustrator.
Title: You can't please everyone/by Ellen Flanagan Burns; illustrated by
Tracy Nishimura Bishop.
Description: Washington, DC: Magination Press, [2022] | Summary: "Ellie feels
like she is disappointing people if she says "no." With help from her parents and
her teacher, she learns how to be honest with people and do the right thing for
herself"—Provided by publisher.
Identifiers: LCCN 2021032389 (print) | LCCN 2021032390 (ebook) | ISBN
9781433839245 (hardcover) | ISBN 9781433839252 (ebook)
Subjects: LCSH: Assertiveness (Psychology)—Juvenile literature. | Self-
confidence—Juvenile literature. | Boundaries (Psychology)—Juvenile literature.
Classification: LCC BF575.A85 B87 2022 (print) | LCC BF575.A85 (ebook) | DDC
158.2—dc23
LC record available at https://lccn.loc.gov/2021032389
LC ebook record available at https://lccn.loc.gov/2021032390
Manufactured in the United States of America
10 9 8 7 6 5 4 3 2 1

Contents

DEAR
Reader

If you're like Ellie, your friends are important to you. It feels good to get along with our friends and have fun. When a friend is feeling down, we're there to listen to them or spend time together. And, it's nice when they do the same for us.

But sometimes the need to make our friends happy or to fit in and be accepted by others can get in the way of our own happiness. We may think things like, "I'll hurt her feelings if I say 'no.' Will he still like me if I don't agree? Maybe I should give in again so she won't be disappointed."

Ellie had worries like these. She was afraid her friends wouldn't like her anymore if she disappointed them in some way. She tried so hard to be liked that she forgot to take care of herself. Over time that left her feeling upset, anxious, and sad.

IT'S NOT YOUR JOB TO:
Please People

When Ellie tries to please people, it feels good at first because it makes them happy, but that good feeling doesn't last very long. Always worrying about what people think is exhausting! Ellie discovers it's much better to just be herself and trust that it's enough for her friends.

Be Liked

The truth is, the way someone feels about you isn't really your concern. The way YOU feel about you is. So, be your best YOU. It's OKAY to be yourself and say "no" to others.

Do It All

Ellie discovers that she can't do it all and besides, her good friends don't expect her to. She feels happier and more confident when she does what feels right instead of what she thinks someone else wants her to do.

IT IS YOUR JOB TO:
Be Kind

Ellie discovers that it feels good to be kind and to help others when she can. That's different than trying to please people. She learns to do the thing that feels right, rather than the thing that makes others like her. When we do what feels right, it gives us a good feeling that lasts.

Be Yourself

There's no one else just like you. That's incredible! Whether you're silly, sweet, quiet, smart, shy, funny, talkative, or outgoing (or all of the above at different times), BE YOU! Ellie relaxes when she discovers that being herself is enough. She learns how to speak up for herself in a way that's friendly *and* true to herself.

Choose Your Friends Wisely

People who expect you to make them happy rather than be yourself can be difficult to get along with. They may blame you when things don't go their way. These kinds of friends can bring out the people-pleasing side of you. Find friends who lift you up, not bring you down. Find friends who like you just the way you are.

Welcome to Ellie's story!

Your friend,
Ellen

Chapter One

PUT ON THE SPOT

Ellie hopped on the bus and wiped the rain from her face. She carefully lowered her umbrella and looked for a place to sit. There was Rosie sitting by herself, staring out the window. She had just moved here and was in Ellie's class in school.

"Hi Rosie!"

"Hi Ellie. You can sit here if you want."

"Thanks." As Ellie sat down, her umbrella popped open, spraying them a little with water. The girls laughed. "Sorry!"

"That's okay."

Ellie was excited about the tetherball tournament coming up next month and she wondered if Rosie ever played. "Did you play tetherball in your last school?" she asked her.

"No, we didn't have it at our school, but I've played before! It's fun!"

Suddenly, from the back of the bus, Sam interrupted, "Hey Ellie, I saved you a seat, come sit with me!" Ellie turned around and saw Sam waving to her. She and Sam were long-time friends. Sam didn't usually ride the bus in the morning, so this was a surprise.

Ellie was happy to see her, but she didn't want to change seats. She was finally settled and besides, she liked getting to know Rosie. She smiled and waved back to Sam, hoping that would be enough to make her happy.

The bus driver closed the door.

Ellie turned back to Rosie. "We play with partners at recess a lot. Do you want to be my partner today, if it ever stops raining?"

"Sure! It'll be fun to play tetherball again."

"We have a few tetherball tournaments every year. There's going to be another one next month," Ellie explained. "I can't wait."

At the next stop, Sam called out again, "Ellie, hurry, come here." When Ellie turned around again, Sam motioned for her to come quickly. Her face looked a little serious. "I need to ask you something."

She's going to keep calling me, Ellie thought. Sam was a good friend, but Ellie had to admit, she could be a little pushy sometimes...like now. She just wanted what she wanted. It would be easier to move seats, Ellie decided.

"Sorry, Rosie, I have to go sit with Sam."

"That's okay," Rosie said. "I'll see you later."

There'll be other chances to sit with Rosie, Ellie thought.

Ellie reached Sam just as the bus pulled away from the stop.

"Hey, what's up?" At first, it felt good making Sam happy, but when Ellie saw Rosie sitting by herself, she felt sad and disappointed in herself for leaving her behind.

"Hey, can you go swimming with me Saturday? I need to know." Sam had asked her on Monday and now it was Thursday, and she still hadn't given her an answer.

Ellie already had plans with her mom Saturday, but she was worried about disappointing Sam. It seemed so important to her. So, instead of saying "no," she had said, "I'll let you know," just to buy some time.

Now she felt put on the spot, the same way she felt when her teacher, Mrs. Iris, called on her to answer a hard math problem. She wasn't sure what to say.

"Well...my mom and I might have plans. We were thinking about painting with my new art supplies...and getting our nails done and going to lunch and..." Ellie paused, hoping Sam would take the hint. She was nervous. Her hands felt clammy. *I hope Sam understands*, she thought.

"Oh," Sam said. She looked disappointed— just what Ellie was afraid of—but she also looked a little confused. "So, can you, or can't you?"

Ellie wanted to say "no" more than anything, but it just wouldn't come out. She hesitated, then shrugged.

"Please?" Sam pushed a little more. "You would have way more fun swimming with me than you would painting with your mom!"

Ellie didn't agree, but it wasn't worth disappointing Sam or starting an argument. Besides, she knew she would have fun swimming too. So, instead she just said "yes."

Sam brightened up. "Thanks, Ellie, you're the best!"

Ellie felt relieved because she made Sam happy. *That was way easier than saying no*, she thought. And she was actually starting to look forward to it. But when she thought of canceling her plans with her mom, the old familiar feelings of sadness and disappointment came back. She stewed quietly for the rest of the ride to school. *There'll be other chances*, she told herself again.

Chapter Two

HEAVY FEELINGS

By recess the rain had stopped and the sun was out. Ellie saw Rosie standing over by the tetherball court, waiting for practice to begin. She joined her.

"Are you ready to play?" she asked Rosie.

"Yes! You're just in time!"

Miss Mary, the teacher at recess, was making the schedule and asked for their team's name.

"Let's call ourselves the Tetherball Tornadoes!" Rosie suggested. Ellie liked it.

It wasn't long before the girls won their first few matches and the Tetherball Tornadoes became the team to beat. They had a good strategy. Since Rosie was taller, she stood behind Ellie and went for the higher balls, while Ellie went for all the lower balls. It was working! Miss Mary announced, "Tetherball Tornadoes are 4 and 0."

The girls high-fived. They were having fun.

While they were waiting for their next match to start, Sam and Jack and a few others from class walked over.

Jack said, "Hey, we need two more players for our softball team. Can we count on you guys?"

"No, we're practicing for the tournament," Rosie explained.

"Yeah, sorry." Ellie felt bad. Jack looked disappointed.

Sam said to Ellie, "But we can't find anyone to play with us." That made Ellie feel even worse, like she was doing something wrong. *Maybe we should play with them*, she thought. She felt torn.

Rosie served to start their next match against Tommy and Billy, who called their team the Baseball Boys, but Ellie was distracted. She missed a few balls, and finally, they lost the game.

"Good practice," Rosie said. "Let's go get lunch."

"Okay. Hey, I wonder if Jack and the others are mad at us," Ellie said.

Rosie didn't understand. "Why would they be mad at us?"

"Because we didn't play softball with them. They needed two more players."

"We were busy. I'm sure they understood. It's okay."

Ellie worried. It didn't feel okay to her.

In the cafeteria, she was having trouble eating lunch. *Jack probably thinks I'm a bad friend... maybe I am*, Ellie thought to herself. She imagined her friends being disappointed in her. She felt as upset as she had that time she invited Sue over for a bike ride and Sam felt left out. She thought she might cry.

Rosie noticed. "Ellie, you haven't touched your pizza." She walked over and gave her a hug. "It's going to be fine," she said gently.

Rosie seemed calm and confident, not worried at all. Ellie wished she could be like that.

"Our plans were just as important as theirs, Ellie," Rosie pointed out. "There's nothing wrong with that."

That's true, Ellie thought. *So why do I feel so bad?* she wondered.

"You know," Rosie added, "you can't please everyone."

∾

When she got home from school, Ellie took out her new watercolor paints. "Mom, can you paint with me?"

"Sure, but I thought we were doing that Saturday before getting our nails done."

"I can't do that anymore. I'm swimming with Sam instead...if she's not mad at me."

"Why would she be mad at you?" her mom wondered.

"Because I didn't play softball with her and Jack." Ellie told her what happened at recess that day.

Her mom listened, then asked, "Well, how do you feel when a friend can't do what you want them to do?"

"I might be disappointed, but..." Ellie's voice faded as she thought it over.

"But, what?"

"But, it's okay," she realized. "They're still my friend."

"And it's the same for you. We all feel disappointed sometimes, but that doesn't mean someone did something wrong, or it's anyone's fault."

Ellie agreed, but she didn't know if Jack and Sam would.

"You could have played softball," her mom said, "but you and Rosie were having fun and besides, you were counting on each other. That's important."

Ellie hadn't thought of it that way. She wasn't used to feeling like her plans were as important as her friends' plans.

She thought about the plans she had with her mom and wondered if her mom was disappointed in her for canceling them. "Mom, were you counting on me too?"

"Well, I *was* looking forward to having fun with you."

"Sorry." Ellie felt bad.

"It's alright. Why don't we get our nails done next Saturday instead?"

Ellie felt relieved. "Thanks, Mom."

"Sure, now let's paint." Ellie's mom was an artist. She'd taught Ellie how to paint with oil, acrylic, and now watercolor. "We use the water to make the colors lighter or darker," she explained, "like this." She dabbed her brush in the pink paint and drew an outline of a rose. "Give it a try and see what you think."

As Ellie was thinking about what to paint, she got a call from Sam. "Hey, I really need your help with our math homework. Can you come over?"

She's not mad at me, Ellie realized. It was a big relief. "Sure, and, sorry about today, I don't even like tetherball that much," she told Sam. It was a little fib. She knew tetherball wasn't Sam's favorite game and she wanted to make her feel better...and most of all she wanted Sam to still like her.

"Oh, that's okay, I'm not upset anymore."

This is my chance to make it up to her, Ellie thought, but then she remembered she was in the middle of something important. "Can you wait an hour?"

"No, I have soccer practice soon. I really need your help now. Please?"

Ellie wanted to say, "This isn't a good time for me," or "I can't right now." But she was so relieved Sam wasn't upset anymore that she said, "I'll be right over."

Sam was happy to hear that. "Thanks, Ellie. I don't know what I would do without you."

On one hand, Ellie was glad she made Sam happy, but on the other hand, she felt frustrated that she couldn't paint anymore and disappointed in herself for canceling her plans with her mom again.

"Mom, I have to go. Sam needs my help with our math homework."

"Why don't you wait until we're done here?"

"Because she has soccer practice soon!" Ellie's voice was louder than usual. She felt frustrated and angry...mostly with herself.

"Well, I won't be able to paint with you later," her mom explained. "I have some things to do."

As Ellie was putting away her brushes, she saw her mom finishing her painting of the rose. She used different shades of pink to make its pretty petals. Ellie felt a pang of sadness and regret. She wished she had said "no" to Sam. She wanted to be painting with her mom more than anything in the world.

Chapter Three

JENNA THE JACKET

When Ellie got home from Sam's, she found her dad in the garage putting away his tools. He had just finished building a rocking chair. The smell of fresh wood filled the air and sawdust covered the floor.

"I think this is my best work yet!" he said. "Go ahead, have a seat!"

Ellie took a seat in the chair and rocked back and forth. She agreed. It was a nice rocking chair.

"The only thing left to do is stain it. I'll have to buy some stain at the hardware store. Now I'm going to clean up here and make some dinner," he said. "How does spaghetti sound?"

Most of the time, Ellie would have loved the idea, but not now. She wasn't feeling very hungry. She shrugged. "That sounds okay, I guess."

"Just okay?" Her dad knew how much she loved spaghetti. "What's wrong?"

"I had a bad day." She told him everything that happened that day starting with the morning bus ride, then worrying about Jack and Sam at recess, and now missing her painting lesson.

Her dad listened as he swept the floor. "That's too bad. You didn't have to do those things, you know."

"I know, but Sam really wanted me to. It's just easier to give in sometimes."

He noticed that disappointing Sam or anyone else really upset Ellie. "You can't please everyone, kiddo. Nobody can. Come on, let's go make dinner."

While they were busy in the kitchen, chopping peppers and onions for the spaghetti sauce, her dad said, "Your day reminds me of a story about a beautiful blue jacket with shiny buttons."

"What's the story?" Ellie asked. She was a little curious.

"Well, this jacket was named Jenna. She was the kind of jacket that was perfect for a spring day. But on rainy days she turned into a silver raincoat to keep her friends dry, and on windy days she turned into a light windbreaker to block the wind, and on cold winter days she became heavier and warmer. If a friend thought she was too small, she stretched herself out to give them room, and if a friend thought she was too big, she made herself small to fit them."

"Cool," Ellie said. "She sounds like a good friend."

"She tried to be, but Jenna just wasn't happy."

"Why not?"

"She was worn out. It was hard work being everything to everyone."

"Oh." Ellie understood that.

"Then one day, a good friend needed her just the way she was."

"A beautiful, blue jacket with shiny buttons." Ellie smiled. "She finally got to be herself."

"Yes. And her friend didn't expect anything else. So, from then on, that's what she was...herself."

Ellie liked that. "But what if someone wanted Jenna to be purple or pink or something else?" she asked.

"Well, it didn't mean she had to be. Being blue was enough."

"Yeah, but what if they didn't like her anymore?" That worried Ellie the most.

"Even though it was nice to be liked, Jenna would rather be herself and besides, she had the kind of friends who liked her just the way she was."

That surprised Ellie a little. Jenna seemed brave.

"When we do things just so someone will like us, or just to make them happy or just to please them, we really aren't being ourselves."

Ellie thought about the way she said "yes," when she wanted to say "no," and telling Sam she didn't like tetherball when she really did, and agreeing with someone just to go along, and all those times she worried about letting her friends down. It didn't feel good. It didn't feel right.

"You don't have to try to make people happy, Ellie. You get to be yourself instead. And that's enough."

Ellie asked, "Even when I disappoint someone, like Jack and Sam today?"

"Yes, even then. We all feel disappointed sometimes."

Ellie remembered how they didn't stay disappointed for very long. "I'm kind of glad I didn't play softball, Dad, because Rosie and I were having fun. And we were counting on each other. I like Rosie."

"I'm glad too. You get to be you, Ellie...the silly, quirky, sweet girl I know. And having good friends, the kind that like you just the way you are, is important. If someone gets mad at you for not doing what they want, or if someone doesn't like you, well then, they aren't your friend anyway. And that's okay, because even a beautiful blue jacket with shiny buttons isn't a good fit for everyone." Her dad smiled.

Being a good friend meant all she had to do was be herself. That felt good to Ellie.

Chapter Four

EMPTY CUP

"Get ready, today we're working on our Native American projects," Mrs. Iris, Ellie's teacher, said. The class had been waiting for this day to arrive and most of them were excited. "Remember to include pictures of arrowheads, descriptions of tools, and samples of artwork," she said. Then she divided the class into groups. "Go ahead and get started. It's due by the end of the day."

It was time to choose a group leader. Ellie looked around at her group. She was pretty good at noticing people and their feelings. Gabe was outgoing and friendly, but sometimes that got in the way of his work. Ellie hoped that wouldn't happen today; they had too much to do. And there was Kyle, who was nice, but a little distracted some days, like today. *I hope he's ready to work*, she thought. And there was Rosie, who was still learning the ropes in her new school.

"I'll be the group leader if you want," Ellie offered.

"Awesome! Thanks," Gabe said. Ellie felt like a hero for a minute.

She divided up the work and they got right to it...or so she thought. When Ellie took a break, she saw Rosie working hard, Kyle playing games on the computer, and Gabe chatting with his friends. She asked the boys for their work and discovered Kyle hadn't even started yet and Gabe hadn't gotten very far. So, Ellie started doing it for them.

"Ellie, you don't have to do *their* work," Rosie said when she saw what happened.

"I know, I'm just trying to help." But deep down, Ellie knew she was being taken advantage of and that made her mad and a little embarrassed. And when she looked at the to-do list, she got a sinking feeling, like she was in a boat filling up with water.

Just then Mrs. Iris came over. She heard the girls talking and looked over at the boys. They got right to work.

Mrs. Iris pulled Ellie aside.

Ellie had a pit in her stomach. She felt like she was caught doing something wrong. "Sorry," she said.

"It's okay," Mrs. Iris said. "This reminds me of the busy barista who worked at Café Chocolate."

Ellie liked going to Café Chocolate, the popular café in town. She usually got ice cream or hot chocolate with whipped cream there.

"People loved the busy barista. 'She does it all,' they said. And she did. She took people's orders, and made them too, all while keeping the place clean. It wasn't unusual for her to make two different drinks at once with brownies baking in the oven! She was *that* good.

"One time a customer came in and ordered four large coffees with cream and sugar, three iced mochas, two hot chocolates, and a large box of cinnamon rolls. He was a nice man, and he wasn't trying to be difficult, but he wanted what he wanted. He assumed she could do it, because she always did. So, the barista got right to work, and the line grew and grew..."

The story gave Ellie a bigger stomachache. "She was doing too much."

"Yes, because she didn't ask for help. It finally caught up to her and she was tired. Her cup felt empty."

Ellie thought of an empty cup of hot chocolate. It had nothing left to give, and that's exactly how she imagined the barista felt right now. Tired! Ellie did too. "Could she hire someone to help?"

"Great idea! That's exactly what she did. She hired someone to work the register, someone to wash the dishes, someone to help make the drinks, and someone to bake the pastries. Once everyone pitched in and did their job, it wasn't so hard. The barista was a lot happier, and her cup felt full again."

Ellie knew where this was going. "I was stuck doing most of the work for my group."

Mrs. Iris nodded. "It's better to share the load."

"But I was just trying to be nice."

"It's important to be nice to yourself too, isn't it?"

Ellie wasn't used to thinking that way, but she had to agree.

Gabe and Kyle approached Ellie and Mrs. Iris. They looked a little sheepish. "Um, Kyle and I just want to say sorry to Ellie for not helping before. We're helping now."

"Thanks guys," Ellie said.

Now that they were doing their part, Ellie's load was lightened and she felt relieved. Her cup felt full again too.

Chapter Five

IT'S NOT *MY* JOB TO PICK *YOUR* ICE CREAM

After dinner that night, Ellie and her parents went to get some ice cream at Café Chocolate. Ellie ordered her usual, blackberry ice cream with a drizzle of peanut butter; her mom ordered strawberry and chocolate ice cream with sprinkles; and her dad ordered his favorite cone, butter pecan, with hot fudge. They found some seats in the back of the café.

Ellie told her parents about what happened at school that day with the project. "I was trying to do Kyle and Gabe's work to be nice, but it was a bad idea," Ellie admitted. "Trying to make them happy made me upset because it wasn't my job."

Her mom nodded. "When we do things just to make someone happy, it means we feel responsible for their feelings," she said.

That was a big idea to Ellie. "I wasn't responsible for how they felt about doing the project. That's impossible!"

Her parents agreed.

"And nobody else is responsible for my feelings. That would be like someone picking my ice cream for me. It's my job."

"Good point!" her dad said.

"I mean, what if they picked butter pecan?" Ellie made a face.

Her dad laughed. "Hey, that's my favorite flavor! But I agree, I wouldn't want someone picking my ice cream either. It's my job."

Ellie went on, "And it would be like crossing an imaginary line during a tetherball match and hitting all of my partner's balls," she said. "That's their job."

Her mom agreed.

Ellie got the giggles thinking of hogging Rosie's balls during a match.

"Or like driving the bus to school for the bus driver," her dad said.

"Or teaching class for Mrs. Iris," her mom added.

Now they all had a case of the giggles.

Ellie could see how these things didn't make sense, how they crossed a line. No wonder she usually ended up feeling frustrated and disappointed or worried and guilty when she tried to please people. And no wonder it left her asking, "Did I do something wrong? Is she mad at me? Am I a bad friend?" She was picking their ice cream for them, and it just wasn't her job.

"I could have reminded Kyle and Gabe that we needed their work soon. That wouldn't have crossed a line," Ellie realized.

"Yeah, and that's a friendly thing to do," her mom agreed.

"And if they still didn't do their work, then I could've just handed in the project without it."

"That makes sense," her dad said.

Ellie announced, "I'm quitting my people pleasing job!"

"Your resignation is accepted!" her mom joked.

Ellie asked, "So, what *is* my job?" Then she remembered Jenna the jacket. "Wait, I know, it's my job to be me."

"And to choose friends who accept you just the way you are," her dad added.

Ellie felt relieved.

Chapter Six

IT'S OKAY TO SAY NO

Ellie finished up her ice cream cone and thought of another tricky situation. Standing up for herself and *saying* "no" when she wanted to was really hard for her. So instead, she usually said "yes," or avoided it altogether. But when she avoided it, it only left people wondering and feeling confused. She remembered when Sam invited her to go swimming on Monday and she didn't answer her until Thursday. It wasn't fair to Sam.

"Mom, sometimes I feel put on the spot," she said. "And it's hard for me to say 'no.' Like when Sam invited me to go swimming, and I already had plans with you."

Ellie's mom understood that feeling. "When I feel that way, I take a breath and remind myself that it's okay to say 'no.' Let's practice it. Pretend you're Sam and I'm you."

Ellie liked this idea. It would be fun playing Sam.

Ellie said, "Hey Ellie, can you come over this weekend and go swimming?"

Ellie's mom responded, "That sounds like fun, Sam, but I already have plans with my mom. Maybe another time."

Ellie liked how her mom answered her. She didn't need to explain herself and it didn't sound mean at all. She wanted to be able to say what she meant just like that, nice and clear. So, she practiced saying it. "That sounds like fun, Sam, but I already have plans with my mom."

"Well done!" her mom said. Her dad agreed.

Ellie noticed it felt good saying what she really meant. It felt kind of natural.

"Let's try another one," her mom said. Ellie's dad was still eating his ice cream, so they had a little more time.

Ellie thought about the time Sam wanted her to switch seats on the bus. So, she said to her mom, "Let's pretend we're on the bus. 'Hey Ellie, come sit with me!'"

"Okay, let's see...you could say something like, 'No, I'm already sitting with someone, but I'll talk to you later, Sam.'"

"'Oh, come on, Ellie!' That's what Sam does, Mom. She can be a little pushy sometimes, you know."

Just then, Ellie's mom turned her body forward and pretended to be talking to Ellie's dad.

Ellie could see what her mom was doing.

"I didn't need to respond anymore," her mom explained. "It's up to Sam to accept my answer and move on."

"But what if Sam felt bad?" Ellie asked. "Or what if she thought I was a bad friend? That's why I moved my seat."

"This sounds like a case of picking Sam's ice cream for her," her dad pointed out. "You really don't have any control over what Sam thinks or feels, do you?"

"No, not unless I just give in and do what she wants." But Ellie knew that wasn't the answer anymore.

Ellie still worried. "This might be really hard."

"It's okay. Doing something hard just takes practice," her mom reassured her, "like learning to paint or learning a new sport. We all get better with practice."

Ellie knew that standing up for herself was the right thing to do, but *not* worrying about people's reactions would take some getting used to. She thought of Jenna the jacket and wondered if she could be so brave...to just be herself. *I think I can,* she thought. Ellie was ready to be herself and be nice to her friends, all at the same time.

Finally, Ellie's mom said, "Let's go home and try the new watercolors."

That made Ellie's day.

∾

When they got home, Ellie got a call from Sam. "Hi Ellie. Can you come over? My dad's starting the firepit and we're making s'mores."

Ellie paused. It sounded like fun, but she would much rather paint with her mom, and besides, her mom was sort of counting on her.

She thought of the last time she said "yes" to Sam when she wanted to say "no," and all the difficult feelings that came from it. This time she was going to be brave and tell her the truth. She started saying, "Maybe...."

Ellie stopped herself. That wasn't clear enough, and it wasn't the way she practiced it with her mom. "I mean..." She took a deep breath, gathered up her courage, and said, "...that sounds like fun, Sam, but I can't right now."

"Why not?"

Ellie could hear Sam's disappointment in her voice. For a moment, the same old thoughts popped in her mind: *I'm not being nice. Sam's going to be disappointed in me. Sam won't like me anymore.* For a moment, she even felt a little guilty and nervous. Then she remembered some new ways of thinking about it: *My plans are important too! I'm a good friend to Sam! Sam will understand!*

She took a breath and said with confidence, "I already have plans with my mom."

"Oh!" Sam said. "What are you doing?"

"We're painting."

"Okay. Have fun, Ellie!"

"Thanks, Sam!"

After she hung up, Ellie felt relieved and a little surprised. Speaking up for herself felt good! She felt confident and lighter without all those heavy feelings weighing her down. And she noticed something else: when she said what she really meant, clearly, Sam didn't try to change her mind.

"Who was that?" her mom asked.

"It was Sam. She invited me over, but I said 'no.' I already have plans with you."

Ellie's mom was proud of her for speaking up and telling Sam the truth. Ellie was too.

"I think she was a little disappointed, but she didn't try to change my mind."

"Well, we all feel disappointed from time to time."

Ellie was doing the right thing for herself and her mom and she was honest with Sam. Sam would choose how she felt about it, and that was fair. It felt good.

She started painting a butterfly. "Hey, this is harder than it looks!"

"It just takes a little practice, like anything else," her mom said. "You'll get the hang of it."

After a few attempts, Ellie finally painted a beautiful butterfly with purple wings.

Chapter Seven
NOT GUILTY

Ellie hopped on the bus and saw Rosie sitting by herself. "Hi, Rosie, can I sit with you?" she asked.

"Sure!" Rosie smiled and moved over.

"Hey, do you want to be my partner for the tetherball tournament next week?" Ellie asked.

"Oh, I can't. Kaelyn and I are going to be partners," Rosie explained. "Sorry." Kaelyn was in their grade, but in a different class.

Ellie felt a little disappointed, but she understood. "Okay."

"What about next time?" Rosie asked. There would be another tournament in a few months.

"Sure!" Ellie noticed that Rosie cared about her feelings, but she didn't seem to feel guilty about saying "no." She just expected Ellie to understand.

Ellie *did* understand. *Rosie's letting me pick my own feelings, my own ice cream*, she realized. *That's fair.*

The bus reached its next stop and Emma hopped on. "Rosie, I have a seat over here, come sit with me!"

Rosie turned around. "Hi Emma!" she called back. "I'm already sitting with Ellie, but I'll talk to you later."

Ellie thought Emma looked disappointed and that made her feel a little uncomfortable, like she was doing something wrong. "Rosie, it's okay if you need to move."

"I don't need to move. I'm already sitting here, with you. Emma will understand."

"But I think she looks disappointed."

"Well, if I moved, then you might be disappointed, or I might be disappointed."

"That's a good point. You can't please everyone, I guess," Ellie said.

Even though Rosie was nice to her friends, she didn't always do what they wanted, Ellie noticed. She did what seemed right to her. And Rosie didn't expect anything different from her friends. It felt good being Rosie's friend. It felt safe.

"Thanks, Rosie. I'm glad you didn't switch seats."

"I am too."

Then Ellie added, "I wish I didn't switch seats on you the other day."

"Oh, that's okay. I really didn't mind that much."

"Thanks, Rosie, but I was taking the easy way out," Ellie admitted. Deep down she knew she would be braver next time.

The girls rode in silence for a while.

Then Rosie said, "Hey, have you noticed how good Tommy and Billy are getting at tetherball?"

"Yes! The Baseball Boys are the best. We have to work on our strategy for the next tournament, when we... I mean the Tetherball Tornados, face them," Ellie said.

The girls talked about their strategy against the boys for the rest of the ride to school.

Chapter Eight

DOING THE *RIGHT* THING, NOT THE *PLEASING* THING

Ellie went with her dad to the hardware store to get some stain for his rocking chair. There was an old man carrying a large bucket of paint in one hand and a two big brushes in the other. He looked like he was having a hard time carrying it all. Ellie's dad ran over and offered to carry the bucket of paint to the checkout counter for him. Ellie offered to carry the brushes. The man was very thankful.

"My back has been bothering me lately," he said. "I should have gotten a cart."

"We're happy to help," her dad said. Once the old man was settled, they waved good-bye to him and off they went to find the stain they needed.

Ellie noticed how good it felt helping the old man. "Why is that different than trying to please people?" she asked her dad.

"Well, let's see...we helped him because he needed it and we were able to. It feels good to be kind to others."

Ellie agreed. It did. "And we *didn't* help him just so he would like us, like Jenna the jacket did," she knew.

"That's true."

"And we *didn't* help him just to make him happy. We weren't trying to pick his feelings for him, or his ice cream." Ellie smiled.

"That's right. We helped him because it felt like the right thing to do, and that always feels good."

Ellie had to agree. She could see the difference. "It's like when you help Grandmom or when Mom volunteers at the senior center, teaching art."

"Yes, we do it because it feels good to give back to people and teaching art is fun for your mom."

"What if she didn't have fun anymore?" Ellie wondered.

"Then she would do something different."

Ellie was happy to hear that her mom took care of herself too. "Would Mom be upset if someone didn't like her art class?"

"No, it's okay when that happens. In fact, it happens all the time. Your mother's satisfaction comes from giving people the opportunity to learn something new, not from whether they like it. When they do like it, it's just icing on the cake."

Ellie's mom and dad didn't do things so people would like them, or just to make them happy, they did things that felt right *and* were true to themselves. Rosie was like that too. Ellie remembered the time Rosie gave her a hug to help her feel better and the time she didn't switch seats on the bus, just because Emma wanted her to. It felt like she *really* cared. She was a good friend.

I'm going to be like that, Ellie decided.

Chapter Nine
FRIENDS FOR LIFE

"Breakfast is ready!" Ellie's mom called.

Ellie grabbed her backpack and ran to the kitchen table. Her bus would be there in 15 minutes.

"The tetherball tournament is today! Finally!" Ellie told her mom as she ate her scrambled eggs.

"Sounds like fun," her mom said. "Who's your partner?"

"I still need one." There were always people who joined the tournament on the day it started, so Ellie wasn't worried about finding a partner.

But Ellie did have a worry. "Sam might want me to play softball with her instead."

"Well, what will you do?"

"I was thinking I could invite her to play tetherball."

"Good idea."

"She might not want to, but...that's her decision."

Her mom agreed.

"Gotta go!" Ellie grabbed her things and ran to catch the bus.

"Have a great day," her mom called after her.

∾

As soon as recess started, Ellie saw a crowd forming over by the tetherball court, so she started heading over.

Just then, Sam ran up and said, "Come on, let's play softball! They need two more players!"

Ellie felt put on the spot, but only for a few seconds. She thought about saying, "maybe," but that would only leave Sam wondering, and that wasn't fair to Sam. Besides, if she said that, Sam would probably try to convince her to play softball even more. She thought about giving in and playing softball just to make Sam happy, but she knew if she did, she would end up feeling frustrated and disappointed in herself.

So, instead she just told her the truth. "That sounds like fun, Sam, but I'm playing in the tetherball tournament today. I've really been looking forward to it."

"I thought you didn't like tetherball." Sam looked surprised.

Ellie felt guilty for telling Sam that she didn't like tetherball when she really did. "The truth is I like tetherball *and* softball. It's just that today is the tetherball tournament, so, if you want, you can play too," Ellie offered.

Ellie started making her way over to the tournament. *Sam's a good friend. She can pick her own feelings*, she thought.

Sam thought about it for a few seconds. "Hey, wait for me, Ellie! I want to play too!"

"Great!" Ellie said.

"Do you want to be my partner?" Sam asked.

"Sure! I need a partner too."

"You're just in time!" Miss Mary said. "What's your team's name?" She was putting the finishing touches on the tournament schedule.

The girls thought hard. "What about Friends for Life?" Ellie suggested.

"I like that! Friends for Life," Sam told Miss Mary.

The tournament was ready to start. Energy was high and there was excitement in the air. Tommy and Billy were the team to beat and everyone knew it.

"Up first on tetherball number one are the Baseball Boys and the Blue Diamonds," Miss Mary announced. The Blue Diamonds were a boy and girl team from class. Miss Mary blew the whistle and play began.

Ellie felt happy. She was being herself *and* being nice all at the same time and it felt good. It felt right. *I'm doing it*, she realized. She saw Rosie in the crowd standing with Kaelyn and waved to her. Rosie waved back with a big smile. Rosie was the kind of friend who liked Ellie just the way she was, and that was special. *There's my other friend for life*, she said to herself.

Ellen Flanagan Burns is a school psychologist and the author of *The Tallest Bridge in the World: A Story for Children About Social Anxiety, Nobody's Perfect: A Story for Children About Perfectionism*, and *Ten Turtles on Tuesday: A Story for Children About Obsessive-Compulsive Disorder*. She devotes her writing to helping children overcome anxiety. She believes that children's books can be a powerful therapeutic tool and supports cognitive-based interventions for children with anxiety-related issues. She lives in Newark, Delaware.

Visit @ellensbooks on Instagram.

Tracy Nishimura Bishop has a degree from San Jose University in graphic design, with a focus on illustration and animation, and is the illustrator of more than 20 children's books. She lives in San Jose, California.

Visit tracybishop.com and @tracybishopart on Instagram and Twitter.

Magination Press is the children's book imprint of the American Psychological Association. APA works to advance psychology as a science and profession and as a means of promoting health and human welfare. Magination Press books reach young readers and their parents and caregivers to make navigating life's challenges a little easier. It's the combined power of psychology and literature that makes a Magination Press book special.

Visit maginationpress.org and @MaginationPress on Facebook, Twitter, Instagram, and Pinterest.